# Snowflake

# Snowflake

By Suzanne Weyn

Illustrated by Jacqueline Rogers

## SCHOLASTIC INC.

New York  Toronto  London  Auckland  Sydney
Mexico City  New Delhi  Hong Kong  Buenos Aires

Thanks to Diana Gonzalez for her help in writing this story.

For Albert, the brave and gentle horse who was
rescued by Diana Gonzalez and Christine Newman.
And for Kelli Wynne of Cimmaron Ranch, who gave
him a home and made his great new life possible.
— S.W.

For Kaleigh and Francis
— J.R.

Library of Congress Cataloging-in-Publication Data.
Weyn, Suzanne.
Snowflake / by Suzanne Weyn ; illustrated by Jacqueline Rogers.
p. cm. Summary: While helping out at Fox Creek Farm, three girls try to find a way to pay
for a new winter blanket needed by a Percheron horse that is new to the stables.
ISBN 0-439-84313-8 (hardcover)
[1. Percheron horse--Fiction. 2. Horses--Fiction.] I. Rogers, Jacqueline, ill. II. Title.
PZ7.W539Sno 2006      [E]--dc22      2005031332

10 9 8 7 6 5                           07 08 09 10/0

Printed in China                        62
First printing, September 2006

# Table of Contents

# At Fox Creek Farm

**E**mily, Anna, and Mandy lived very close to Fox Creek Farm. After school, the three friends liked to help with the horses and the other animals that lived on the farm.

Kelly and Chris were sisters who owned the farm. They kept horses and gave riding lessons. They also took in animals that had no home.

One day, Emily, Anna, and Mandy saw a new horse at the farm. He was very big. He looked dirty and thin. And his mane was messy. He seemed sad.

Mandy, Anna, and Emily petted the horse.

"He's so skinny, I can feel his bones," said Mandy. "Where did he come from?"

"His owners left him behind when they moved to the city," said Kelly. "So the animal

officer brought him here just for a little while. We'll have to find him a new home."

"Why can't we keep him?" Emily asked.

"I'm afraid we have no more stalls in the stable," Chris told the girls. "He's so big, he might even need two stall spaces."

"You could put him in the open paddock," Emily said. "In nature, horses live outside."

"And we would feed him and groom him," Anna said.

"I don't know," said Chris. Kelly and Chris spoke to each other quietly.

"Emily, Anna, Mandy, and Chris, take him to the wash stall for a bath. He's ours!" Kelly said.

"Yay!" the girls cheered.

As they washed the new horse, the girls were sure they could make him healthy and strong once again.

## Chapter 2

# First Snow

**W**eeks passed. The first snow flurries fell. The girls named the new horse Snowflake. They groomed him, watered him, and fed him. They brought him apples and carrots. Soon his ribs no longer showed.

Snowflake was happy. He liked his new friends. He whinnied to the girls whenever they came to see him.

One day, when Snowflake was strong
enough, Kelly started to hand-walk him for
exercise. Sometimes she let the girls ride him
bareback while she walked him.

"Snowflake is a Percheron," Kelly told
the girls. "Percherons are draft horses, often
used for farmwork and driving," she said.
"And someone did a good job of training
Snowflake. He obeys voice commands
so well."

It was getting cold. Many owners put warm blankets on their horses at night. "Let's go ask Chris and Kelly if they have an extra blanket," Emily said.

Kelly could find only a thin, worn horse blanket. When Anna tried to put the blanket on Snowflake, it was too small. The straps didn't reach under him. The blanket slid off every time he moved.

The next day, the girls looked at a
catalog of horse gear. A warm blanket big
enough for Snowflake would cost a lot of
money. The girls put all their money together.
They didn't have enough.

"We have to find a way to get him a bigger and warmer blanket," Emily said. "I don't want him to freeze on these cold nights."

# A Surprise in the Barn

In December, the farm became an even busier place. Many friends came to help Chris and Kelly decorate for their yearly winter festival. The sisters used the money they made at the festival to help feed their animals.

Anna, Emily, and Mandy helped to set up, too. Chris asked them to go to the old barn and find a box of horseshoes in there. "We need them for the horseshoe toss game," she said.

The girls had never been to the old barn. They were eager to look inside. As they ran, big snowflakes began to fall.

The barn was full of old tack, gear, and tools. The girls almost forgot about the horseshoes as they looked around.

"Come see what I found!" Mandy called from the back of the barn. Anna and Emily went to join her.

It was an old sleigh, made for a horse. Two people could sit in front, and a few more could sit in the back.

"It's just like in the song 'Jingle Bells!'"
Anna said. "It's a one-horse open sleigh!"

Mandy saw a trunk next to the sleigh
and opened it. Inside was a large, heavy
harness.

"Look! Here are the jingle bells," said
Mandy, shaking the harness. "Real jingle bells!"

"I know how to get a blanket for
Snowflake!" Emily cried.

# A Great Idea — Maybe!

They raced from the old barn to find Chris and Kelly. Snowflake nickered as the girls ran past.

"We want to use the sleigh to give rides at the winter festival!" shouted Emily. "We can use the money we make to buy Snowflake his horse blanket!"

"I almost forgot about that old sleigh,"
Chris said.

"It belonged to our great-grandparents,"
said Kelly. "I don't think you can use it, though.
We don't have a horse that can pull a sleigh."

"I bet Snowflake could do it," Chris said.

"He's a draft horse."

They all looked at Snowflake.

"Maybe," Kelly said. "He is well trained. We'll have to try him. But first, we have to clean that sleigh!"

Mandy was so excited that she shook the bells. Snowflake's ears pricked forward in interest. "He likes the bells," she said, pointing to his ears. "He's heard them before!"

# The Winter Festival

The next day, friends helped them get the sleigh out of the barn. The sleigh slid easily on the newly fallen snow. Once it was outside, the girls cleaned and polished the sleigh. It was beautiful.

Kelly and Chris bridled Snowflake. Then they hitched him to the sleigh. Snowflake looked very happy.

Kelly sat in the driver's seat. She made a
clucking sound, telling Snowflake to go. But
he just stood there.

"I don't think he knows what to do,"
Chris said.

Mandy climbed in beside Kelly. Kelly shook the reins, ringing the bells. Snowflake nodded and whinnied. He began to move! "He can do it!" Mandy cheered.

The following week was the winter festival. And Snowflake was the star! Everyone wanted to ride in a real one-horse open sleigh, with its jingling bells. Snowflake was happy, too. He loved pulling the sleigh through the snow.

All winter long, people wanted rides in the sleigh. The girls made lots of money. They bought Snowflake a bright red, winter horse blanket that was very warm. There was enough money for Kelly and Chris to build a run-in shed for Snowflake in the paddock. Anna, Kelly, and Mandy no longer worried about their horse. Snowflake was safe, warm, and happy in his new home!

# About Percherons

## Facts about Percherons:

1. Percherons are originally from Le Perche, near Normandy, France.

2. Percherons were once used on many farms in America, until the modern farm tractor was invented.

3. Today, Percherons are used on small farms and for sleigh rides, hayrides, and parades.

4. Percherons range in height from 15 to 19 hands, with most being between 16.2 and 17.3 hands. A hand is four inches high.

5. The Percheron Horse Association of America registers about 2,500 new foals each year.

When Horses Are All You Dream About...

## It has to be Breyer® model horses!

Breyer® model horses are fun to play with and collect!
Meet horse heroes that you know and love. Learn about horses
from foreign lands. Enjoy crafts and games.
Visit us at **www.BreyerHorses.com/kidsbooks**
for horse fun that never ends!